S0-AJG-960

Childsworld 4/19
19.95

U.S.A. TRAVEL GUIDES

Hawai'i

BY ANN HEINRICHS • ILLUSTRATED BY MATT KANIA

The Child's World®
childsworld.com

Published by The Child's World®
1980 Lookout Drive • Mankato, MN 56003-1705
800-599-READ • www.childsworld.com

Photo Credits
Photographs ©: iStockphoto, cover, 1, 11, 35; J. Wei/
National Park Service, 7; Brenda Zaun/USFWS, 8;
Nigel Hicks/DK Images, 12; Library of Congress, 14, 18;
Daniel Ramirez CC2.0, 15, 20, 28; Tess Heder CC2.0,
16; Rob Reichenfeld/DK Images, 19; Andre Jenny Stock
Connection Worldwide/Newscom, 23; randychiu CC2.0,
24; Mass Communication Specialists 3rd Class Diana
Quinlan/U.S. Navy, 27; National Park Service, 31; Tavis
Jacobs CC2.0, 32; Zvonimir Atletic/Shutterstock Images,
34; Shutterstock Images, 37 (left), 37 (right).

Copyright
Copyright © 2018 by The Child's World®
All rights reserved. No part of this book may be
reproduced or utilized in any form or by any means
without written permission from the publisher.

ISBN 9781503819511
LCCN 2016961173

Printing
Printed in the United States of America
PA02334

Ann Heinrichs is the author of more than 100 books for children and young adults. She has also enjoyed successful careers as a children's book editor and an advertising copywriter. Ann grew up in Fort Smith, Arkansas, and lives in Chicago, Illinois.

post card

About the Author
Ann Heinrichs

Matt Kania loves maps and, as a kid, dreamed of making them. In school he studied geography and cartography, and today he makes maps for a living. Matt's favorite thing about drawing maps is learning about the places they represent. Many of the maps he has created can be found in books, magazines, videos, Web sites, and public places.

post card

About the
Map Illustrator
Matt Kania

On the cover: Waiʻānapanapa State Park has a black sand beach.

OUR HAWAI'I TRIP

HAWAI'I

Are you ready to explore the Aloha State? Then hop aboard. We're heading out to Hawai'i!

You'll surf ocean waves. You'll learn a new way to crack nuts. You'll even climb a **volcano** and eat roasted pig. Does that sound like fun? Then buckle up and hang on tight. We're off!

WELCOME TO HAWAI'I

Hawai'i's Nickname: The Aloha State

Aloha is a Hawai'ian word meaning "kindness" or "love." It's used to say hello or goodbye.

As you travel through Hawai'i, watch for all the interesting facts along the way.

PACIFIC OCEAN

Ni'ihau

Kilauea Point Refuge

Kaua'i

Kaumakani

Līhu'e

O'ahu

Wahiawa

Lā'ie

H2

H1

H3

Pearl Harbor

Honolulu

HAWAI'I

Moloka'i

Kualapu'u

Kalaupapa

Lāna'i City

Lāna'i

Lahaina

Maui

Hāna

Kaho'olawe

Kupa'au

Hawai'i

Hilo

PACIFIC OCEAN

Many Hawai'ian words have diacritics, or special marks. One is the 'okina ('). It tells you to stop the breath quickly in your throat. The kahakō, or macron (¯), means you should make a vowel sound longer.

HAWAI'I VOLCANOES NATIONAL PARK

You're in Hawai'i Volcanoes National Park. Steamy clouds pour out of the ground. Lava, or melted rock, glows fiery red. Stay clear! The lava and steam are dangerous!

Hawai'i is way out in the Pacific Ocean. It's made up of more than 130 islands! There are eight main islands. The biggest is the island of Hawai'i. It's often called the Big Island. The others are O'ahu, Maui, Lāna'i, Kaua'i, Moloka'i, Kaho'olawe, and Ni'ihau.

Hawai'i's islands are actually the tops of volcanoes. Lava once poured out of them. The rock cooled and formed the islands. Most of these volcanoes are now **dormant**. But some are still smoking away!

Don't miss the lava lake in Halema'uma'u Crater.

KĪLAUEA POINT NATIONAL WILDLIFE REFUGE

You're exploring Kīlauea Point National Wildlife Refuge. That's on the north coast of the island of Kauaʻi. Suddenly you hear a soft, honking call. It's a nēnē, or Hawaiʻian goose.

Many seabirds nest along Hawaiʻi's coasts. Huge sea turtles nest there, too. Whales, seals, and dolphins swim offshore.

Many islands have rugged mountains. Waterfalls plunge down the rocky hillsides. Deep forests stretch for miles. They're home to frogs, lizards, and birds.

Many food plants grow wild in Hawaiʻi. These include papaya, banana, and coconut palm trees. Plumeria and other beautiful flowers are everywhere.

This nēnē lives in Kīlauea Point National Wildlife Refuge. The nēnē is an endangered species.

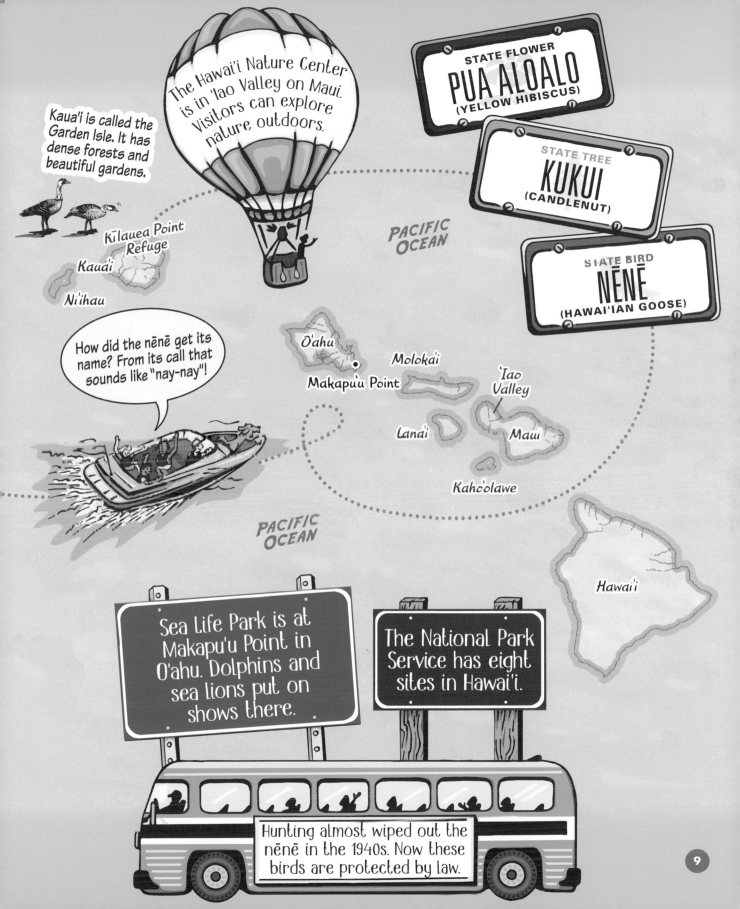

The first free public library in Hawai'i opened in Honolulu in 1913.

Hang five! You're in the soup! Don't wipe out!

PACIFIC OCEAN

Kaua'i

Ni'ihau

O'ahu

★ Honolulu

Moloka'i

Lāna'i

Maui

Kaho'olawe

PACIFIC OCEAN

Hawai'i

Surfing Terms:
hang five to surf with five toes curled around the front of the surfboard
in the soup in the wave's foam after the wave has broken
wipe out to fall off your surfboard

Surfing used to be a sport for Hawai'i's **royalty**.

The Bishop Museum in Honolulu features plants, animals, and **archaeological** discoveries specific to the islands. Western art and Asian art are found at the Honolulu Museum of Arts.

SURFING ON O'AHU'S COAST

The waves rise higher than a house. They crash with a thundering roar! This is O'ahu's northern coast. The world's biggest surfing contests are held here.

Surfing is a favorite sport in Hawai'i. People love sunning on the beaches, too. Honolulu's Waikīkī Beach is popular for both of these. Honolulu is located on O'ahu's southern coast.

Aloha Festivals is a big event in Hawai'i. It runs throughout September. People celebrate with feasts, parades, and **hula** dancing.

Sports bring many visitors to Hawai'i. Honolulu hosts the Hawai'i Bowl in late December. It's a college football game. The Ironman World Championship happens on Hawai'i island. Athletes swim through the ocean. They bike over lava fields. They run along scenic roads.

Experienced surfers enjoy the challenge of the Banzai Pipeline off O'ahu's north shore.

Climb a certain hillside on the island of Lāna'i. Big rocks are scattered on the hill. They're carved with almost 1,000 amazing pictures! There are people, goats, dogs, and turtles. There are scenes of battles and hunts.

These are the Luahiwa Petroglyphs near Lāna'i City. Petroglyphs are words or pictures carved in rock. Early Hawai'ians carved them hundreds of years ago.

Polynesians were the first people in Hawai'i. They arrived about 1,500 years ago. They came from faraway islands.

Captain James Cook sailed to Hawai'i in 1778. This British explorer was the first European in Hawai'i. Soon, many other explorers and traders came.

Some of the Luahiwa Petroglyphs have been damaged as tourists have carved into the rocks themselves.

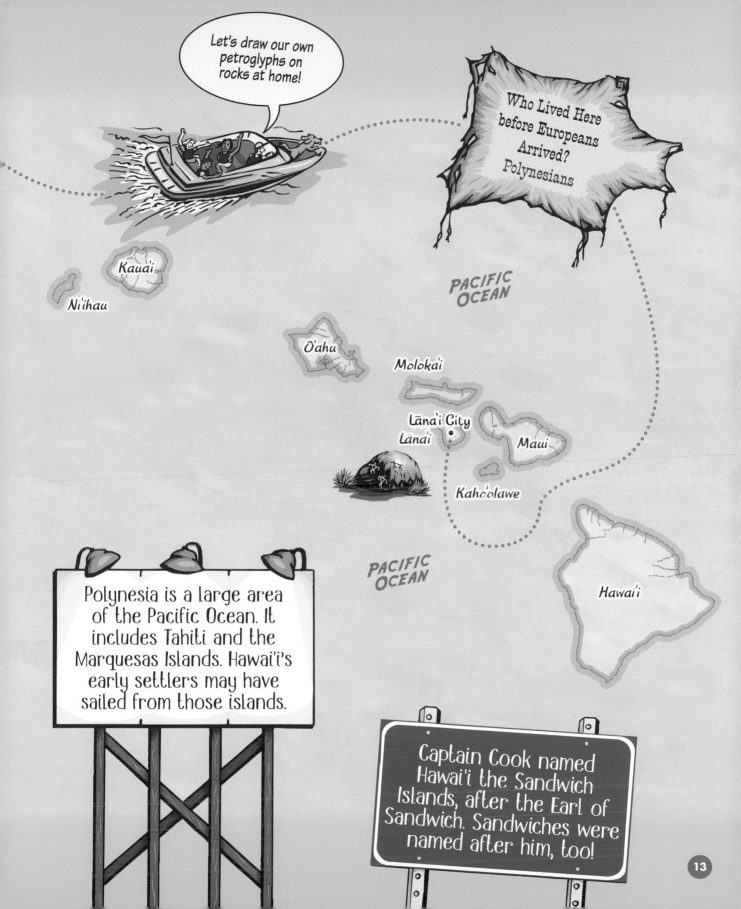

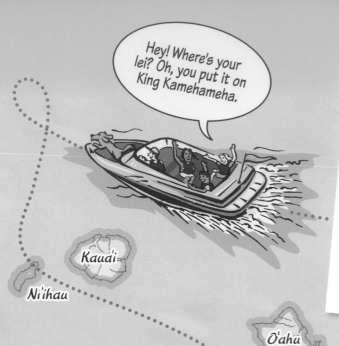

Hey! Where's your lei? Oh, you put it on King Kamehameha.

Your Majesty:
You traded Hawai'i's sandalwood with China. That made your kingdom rich. You also brought peace to the islands and made laws to protect the common people. No wonder they call you Kamehameha the Great!

Sincerely,
A. Kahuna

King Kamehameha I
1758?-1819
Hawai'i Island, HI

Kaua'i

Ni'ihau

O'ahu

Molokai

PACIFIC OCEAN

Lāna'i

Maui

PACIFIC OCEAN

Kaho'olawe

• Kapa'au

Hawai'i

It's a Hawai'ian custom to welcome or honor people by draping leis around their necks.

Hawai'i's native religion included holy men called kahunas. They were known for curing sickness and seeing into the future. The kahunas predicted Kamehameha's rise to power.

Kapa'au's Kamehameha statue was made in Europe. It was sent by ship to Hawai'i in 1880. The ship sank, and the statue was lost. Later, it was recovered and brought to Kapa'au.

Girls on horseback parade down the street. Everyone's wearing a lei, which is a necklace of flowers. But one figure has more leis than anyone else. It's the statue of King Kamehameha I.

You're in Kapa'au, on the island of Hawai'i. And it's June 11. That's King Kamehameha Day!

King Kamehameha I was a great leader. He united Hawai'i into one kingdom in 1795. Europeans were beginning to explore the islands. But King Kamehameha kept his kingdom strong and free.

All of Hawai'i celebrates King Kamehameha Day. People in Kapa'au are very proud that day. The king was born near their town.

Hawai'ians have celebrated King Kamehameha Day since 1871.

HĀNA CULTURAL CENTER ON MAUI

Francis "Tito" Marciel Wilhelmina "Mina" Marciel

Maria Tallant Marciel

You see stone lamps and coconut graters. You see fishhooks made of seashells. You see curved poi boards, too. Hawai'ians pounded cooked taro root on these boards. That's how they made a food called poi.

You're visiting Hāna Cultural Center on Maui. It **preserves** an early Hawai'ian community. Several hale, or houses, stand there. They show much about Hawai'ian life throughout history.

Protestant **missionaries** from Boston, Massachusetts, arrived in 1820. The Hawai'ians' way of life changed. The missionaries made a writing system for the Hawai'ian language. Hawai'ians began to dress like Americans and Europeans. Still, Hawai'ians also kept some ancient customs. Many new settlers adopted Hawai'ian customs, too.

At the Hāna Cultural Center, you will see photos in memory of people who were part of Hāna's community.

Early Hawai'ians ate poi, fish, sweet potatoes, breadfruit, and coconut. Hawai'ians still eat these foods today.

PACIFIC OCEAN

Kaua'i

Ni'ihau

O'ahu

Molokai

Lāna'i

Maui • Hāna

I think we need some lomilomi sticks. They're great for back rubs!

Kaho'olawe

Hawai'i

PACIFIC OCEAN

Poi is a thick paste made from taro root.

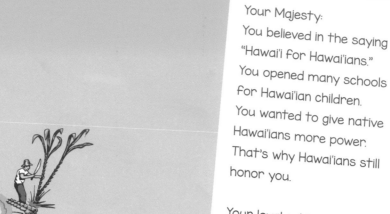

Your Majesty:
You believed in the saying "Hawai'i for Hawai'ians."
You opened many schools for Hawai'ian children.
You wanted to give native Hawai'ians more power.
That's why Hawai'ians still honor you.

Your loyal subject,
Robert Wilcox

post card

Queen Lili'uokalani
1838-1917
Honolulu, HI

Kaua'i
• Līhu'e

Ni'ihau

Polynesian people brought in Hawai'i's first sugarcane plants.

Wow! I didn't know sugar comes from a plant!

O'ahu

★
Honolulu

Molokai

Lāna'i

Maui

Kaho'olawe

PACIFIC OCEAN

PACIFIC OCEAN

Hawai'i

Queen Lili'uokalani lived in Honolulu's 'Iolani Palace. It was built by her brother, King Kālakaua.

Queen Lili'uokalani was Hawai'i's only queen. She was the last ruler of the Kingdom of Hawai'i.

Sugarcane stalks are pressed to squeeze out a thick, sweet juice. That juice yields molasses and raw sugar.

GROVE FARM SUGAR PLANTATION MUSEUM ON KAUA'I

Take a tour of Grove Farm Sugar Plantation Museum in Līhu'e. It's a 100-acre (40-hectare) plantation on the island of Kaua'i. You'll see a banana patch and the plantation office. The museum teaches about Hawai'i's sugarcane history. Hawai'i grew sugar from 1835 to 2016.

Americans and Europeans started Hawai'i's first plantations. They opened sugarcane plantations in the 1830s. Pineapple plantations were opened in the 1880s.

Queen Lili'uokalani came to power in 1891. But planters and other foreigners were powerful, too. They led a revolution in 1893. Lili'uokalani was removed from the throne. Then Hawai'i became the Republic of Hawai'i. It became a U.S. territory in 1900.

Relax on the Grove Farm's koa wood veranda.

THE POLYNESIAN CULTURAL CENTER ON O'AHU

Toss a spear and crack a coconut. Try an ancient form of bowling. You're at the Polynesian Cultural Center! It has many villages. Each one features the **culture** of a Polynesian island.

Polynesian people were the first Hawai'ians. Hawai'ians developed their own language. Today, many Hawai'ian words are still used in Hawai'i. Native Hawai'ian food and music are common, too.

Now people from many countries live in Hawai'i. Planters brought in **immigrants** to work their farms. These workers came from China, Japan, Portugal, and other lands. They all brought different customs with them. Now these customs are part of Hawai'ian life.

Check out the Tahiti village at the Polynesian Cultural Center. You might catch some beautiful dancing!

Oh, boy! Let's get a Marquesan tattoo! Don't worry, Mom. It can be washed off.

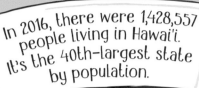

In 2016, there were 1,428,557 people living in Hawai'i. It's the 40th-largest state by population.

PACIFIC OCEAN

Niʻihau

Kauaʻi

- Lāʻie
Oʻahu
- Kailua
★
Honolulu

Molokaʻi

Lānaʻi

Maui

PACIFIC OCEAN

Kahoʻolawe

Hilo •
Hawaiʻi
• Hōnaunau

Population of Largest Cities
Honolulu....................350,399
Hilo..........................43,263
Kailua........................38,635

Oʻahu has the highest population of all the islands. It's home to about three out of four people in Hawaiʻi.

Hawaiʻi's Puʻuhonua o Hōnaunau National Historical Park is near the town of Hōnaunau. It teaches visitors the history of the Polynesian people.

The Polynesian Cultural Center is in Lāʻie, on the island of Oʻahu. It highlights the cultures of Hawaiʻi, Samoa, New Zealand, Fiji, Tahiti, Tonga, and the Marquesas.

PURDY'S MACADAMIA NUT FARM ON MOLOKA'I

Put that macadamia nut in a sock. That way, you won't hurt your fingers. Then smash it with a hammer. Whack!

You're visiting Purdy's Macadamia Nut Farm. It's near Kualapu'u on the island of Moloka'i. The Purdys are happy to show you around. They'll teach you stuff, too. Like how to crack a macadamia nut!

People in Hawai'i grow lots of unusual crops. Pineapple is a major crop. Pineapples mostly grow on the island of Maui.

Farmers also raise nuts, coffee, and flowers. Many delicious fruits grow in Hawai'i, too. Bananas, mangoes, and papayas are just a few. And you don't need a hammer to eat them!

Purdy's Macadamia Nut Farm has hundreds of macadamia trees on 5 acres (2 ha) of land.

DOLE PLANTATION'S PINEAPPLE GARDEN MAZE

Turn left, turn right, go straight. Oops! A dead end!

You're at Dole Plantation near Wahiawā on Oʻahu. Farmers there grow pineapples. And you're in the Pineapple Garden **Maze**. It's the biggest maze in the world. Don't get lost!

You can tour this plantation in a little train. You'll see its store, too. It's full of pineapple products.

Foods are Hawaiʻi's major factory products. Crops such as pineapples go from farms to factories. There they might be squeezed, chopped, or cooked. Fruits become fruit juice, soft drinks, or jam. Some crops end up as candy. Yum!

You'll see many pineapple plants at the Dole Plantation. You can buy fresh pineapple!

Hawai'i was the 50th state to enter the Union. It joined on August 21, 1959.

PACIFIC OCEAN

The Arizona's anchor is in the visitor center. It weighs 19,585 pounds (8,884 kg).

Kaua'i

Ni'ihau

O'ahu

Pearl Harbor

Moloka'i

Lāna'i

Maui

Kaho'olawe

Look at that monster anchor! It weighs as much as several elephants!

PACIFIC OCEAN

Hawai'i

The Japanese attacked Pearl Harbor on December 7, 1941.

Look down through the clear blue water. You can see a sunken ship down there. It's the battleship USS *Arizona*.

You're visiting the USS *Arizona* Memorial. It's at Pearl Harbor on the island of O'ahu. Japan bombed the U.S. base there in 1941. The *Arizona* sank, and many people died. Then the United States entered World War II (1939–1945).

Hawai'i grew quickly after the war ended. Tourism became a big business. Now millions of people visit Hawai'i every year. They enjoy the state's natural beauty and warm climate.

Visitors must reach the memorial by boat. Part of the USS Arizona *is visible above the water.*

THE STATE CAPITOL IN HONOLULU

You've never seen a state capitol like Hawai'i's. It was built with a volcano in mind! The top is open to the sky. That's what craters look like. Some rooms are cone-shaped—just like volcanoes. What a great home for state government offices!

Hawai'i's state government has three branches. One branch makes laws for the state. The governor heads another branch. It makes sure people obey the laws. Judges make up the third branch. They decide whether laws have been broken.

The center of the capitol building is open to the sky, as if visitors were inside a volcano.

Haleakalā's crater is more than 7 miles (11 km) across.

PACIFIC OCEAN

Kaua'i

Ni'ihau

O'ahu

Moloka'i

Lāna'i

Maui   Haleakalā Volcano

Kaho'olawe

The crater at the top of Haleakalā is Maui's highest point.

Don't worry! Haleakalā is dormant. It has not erupted for hundreds of years.

Hawai'i

Ancient Hawai'ian legends say that the Sun sleeps in Haleakalā's giant crater.

PACIFIC OCEAN

Haleakalā is the only place on Earth where the silversword plant grows.

CLIMBING MAUI'S HALEAKALĀ VOLCANO

You're hiking up Haleakalā volcano. It's very early in the morning. You're bundled up because it's so cold. Suddenly, rays of light burst out. The Sun has risen!

Haleakalā is Hawai'ian for "house of the Sun." People like to drive to the top of this volcano at sunrise. They watch the sky turn beautiful colors.

At the top, you'll explore the crater. It's one of the largest dormant volcanic craters in the world. It was formed by erosion. Hiking across it can take many days!

Explore the rugged trails in the Haleakalā crater.

A LŪʻAU AT LAHAINA

Tables of food seem to stretch for miles. They're loaded with chicken, salmon, and squid. There's every color of fruit and vegetable. In the middle is a big roasted pig.

You're enjoying a lūʻau. That's a huge Hawaiʻian feast. This one's at Lahaina on Maui's west coast. Its lūʻaus are famous.

Big feasts are an old Hawaiʻian **tradition**. They were held to celebrate special events. Today's lūʻaus usually include a show. There are hula dances with traditional music. Some shows tell the history of the Hawaiʻian people. So a lūʻau is much more than just a meal!

At dark, visitors can enjoy both traditional and contemporary hula dancing.

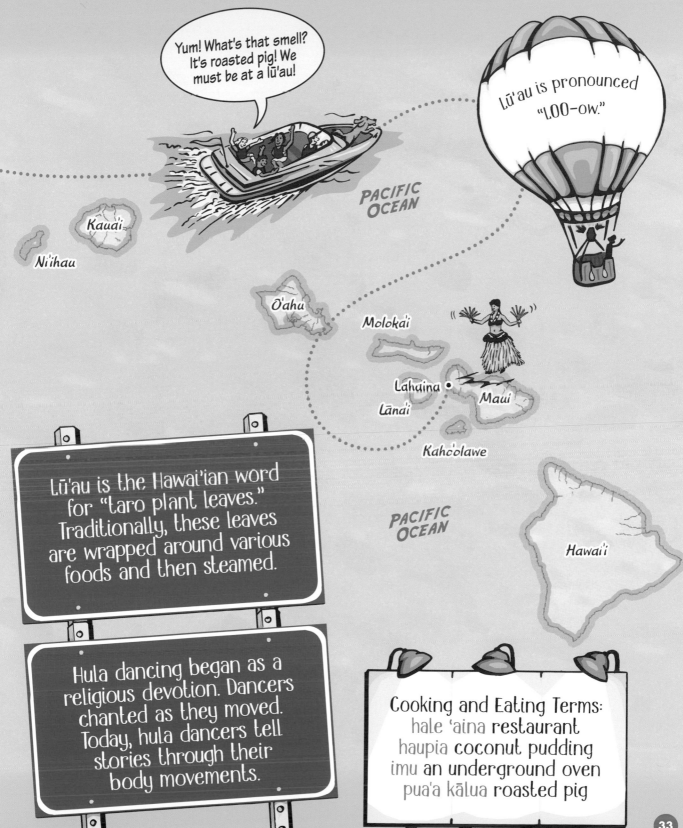

Lū'au is the Hawai'ian word for "taro plant leaves." Traditionally, these leaves are wrapped around various foods and then steamed.

Hula dancing began as a religious devotion. Dancers chanted as they moved. Today, hula dancers tell stories through their body movements.

Cooking and Eating Terms:
hale 'aina restaurant
haupia coconut pudding
imu an underground oven
pua'a kālua roasted pig

Hansen's disease affects the skin, nerves, and muscles. It can now be cured with medicine. Hansen's disease used to be called leprosy.

Are you sure this mule knows what it's doing? It's mighty far down to the sea!

PACIFIC OCEAN

Ni'ihau

Kaua'i

O'ahu

Guides who manage the mules are called mule skinners.

• Kalaupapa

Moloka'i

Lāna'i

Maui

Kaho'olawe

PACIFIC OCEAN

Hawai'i

Dear Father Damien:
People with Hansen's disease were treated badly. No one wanted to be near them. But you helped ease their pain. Then you died of the disease yourself. What a good person you were!

Sincerely,
An Admirer

post card

Father Damien
1840-1889
Kalaupapa, Moloka'i

The Hawai'ian government began sending people with Hansen's disease to Moloka'i in 1866.

Father Damien was a Roman Catholic priest from Belgium. His full name was Joseph Damien de Veuster. He came to Kalaupapa in 1873.

RIDING MULES ON THE CLIFFS OF MOLOKAʻI

Your mule's name is Friendly. But you wish his name were Steady. You're riding him along Molokaʻi's northern cliffs. They're the highest sea cliffs in the world!

Soon you reach the village of Kalaupapa. It was once a village for sick people. They all had Hansen's disease. A priest called Father Damien cared for them. Many people were afraid they would catch the disease. But Father Damien was brave. The sick people loved him for his kindness.

Now you're back on your mule. This time, you're not afraid. Friendly is very steady on those cliffs!

Erosion carved valleys among the Molokaʻi cliffs.

OUR TRIP

We visited many places on our trip! We also met a lot of interesting people along the way. Look at the map below. Use your finger to trace all the places we have been.

Which island has "barking sand"? *See page 6 for the answer.*

Which islands does Polynesia include? *Page 13 has the answer.*

What is poi? *See page 17 for the answer.*

Who was Hawai'i's only queen? *Look on page 18 for the answer.*

How many macadamia nuts does Hawai'i grow? *Page 22 has the answer.*

When was Pearl Harbor attacked? *Turn to page 26 for the answer.*

Where does the silversword plant grow? *Look on page 30 and find out!*

What is another name for Hansen's disease? *Turn to page 34 for the answer.*

PACIFIC OCEAN

Ni'ihau

Kaua'i
Kilauea Point Refuge
Kaumakani
Lihu'e

La'ie
Wahiawa
O'ahu
H2
H1
H3
Pearl Harbor
Honolulu

HAWAI'I

Moloka'i
Kualapu'u
Kalaupapa

Lāna'i City
Lāna'i

Kaho'olawe

Lahaina
Maui
Hāna

Kapa'au

Hawai'i

Hilo

PACIFIC OCEAN

STATE SYMBOLS

State bird: Nēnē (Hawai'ian goose)

State dance: Hula

State fish: Humuhumunukunukuāpua'a (rectangular triggerfish)

State flower: Pua aloalo (yellow hibiscus)

State gem: Black coral

State individual sport: Surfing

State marine mammal: Humpback whale

State team sport: Outrigger canoe paddling

State tree: Kukui (candlenut)

State seal

STATE SONG

"HAWAI'I PONO'Ī" ("HAWAI'I'S OWN")

Words by King David Kalākaua, music by Henry Berger

In Hawai'ian:
Hawai'i pono'ī
Nānā i kou, mō'ī
Ka lani ali'i,
Ke ali'i.

In English:
Hawai'i's own true sons
Be loyal to your chief
Your country's liege and lord
The chief.

Hui:
Makua lani ē,
Kamehameha ē,
Nā kaua e pale,
Me ka ihe.

Chorus:
Royal father
Kamehameha
Shall defend in war
With spears.

I Hawai'i pono'ī
Nānā i nā ali'i
Nā pua muli kou
Nā pōki'i.

Hawai'i's own true sons
Look to your chief
Those chiefs of younger birth
Younger descent.

Hawai'i pono'ī
E ka lāhui e
'O kāu hana nui
E ui e.

Hawai'i's own true sons
People of loyal heart
The only duty lies
List and abide.

That was a great trip! We have traveled all over Hawai'i! There are a few places that we didn't have time for, though. Next time, we plan to visit the Pacific Tsunami Museum in Hilo. This museum educates visitors about giant and destructive sea waves. It features exhibits on tsunami safety and the history of tsunamis in Hawai'i.

State flag

FAMOUS PEOPLE

Ariyoshi, George (1926–), governor

Atisanoe, Salevaa (Konishiki) (1963–), sumo wrestler

de Veuster, Joseph Damien (1840–1889), missionary

Fong, Hiram L. (1906–2004), senator

Graham, Lauren (1967–), actor

Hamilton, Bethany (1990–), surfer and actor

Higa, Ryan (1990–), YouTube star and actor

Ho, Don (1930–2007), singer

Inaba, Carrie Ann (1968–), actor, choreographer, *Dancing with the Stars* judge

Kahanamoku, Duke Paoa (1890–1968), Olympic swimmer, surfing pioneer

Kamakawiwoʻole, Israel (1959–1997), singer

Kidman, Nicole (1967–), actor

Liliʻuokalani, Queen Lydia (1838–1917), Hawaiʻian queen

Lowry, Lois (1937–), children's author

Mars, Bruno (1985–), singer

Obama, Barack (1961–), 44th president of the United States

Onizuka, Ellison S. (1946–1986), astronaut

Tuttle, Merlin (1941–), ecologist and wildlife photographer

Wacker, Ethan (2002–), actor who lives in Hawaiʻi

Wie, Michelle (1989–), golfer

WORDS TO KNOW

archaeological (ar-kee-uh-LA-juh-kuhl) relating to the study of the remains of past cultures

culture (KUHL-chur) a group of people's beliefs, customs, and way of life

dormant (DOR-muhnt) not active; sleeping

hula (HOO-luh) a Hawaiʻian dance performed with swaying movements

immigrants (IM-uh-gruhnts) people who leave their home country and move to another land

legends (LEJ-uhndz) old tales created to explain something

maze (MAYZ) a confusing set of pathways

missionaries (MISH-uh-nair-eez) people who travel somewhere to spread their faith

preserves (pri-ZURVZ) protects something so that it remains unchanged

royalty (ROI-uhl-tee) kings, queens, and other nobles

tradition (truh-DISH-uhn) custom

volcano (vol-KAY-noh) a mountain that releases steam and melted rock